THE
DRAGON BONE FLUTE

A Novella by:
M. Todd Gallowglas

M Todd Gallowglas

For Penny
For helping me see past my rough drafts to the real stories I want to tell.

The Dragon Bone Flute

I

If any one moment could be said to be the turning point in my life, the moment where destiny shifted, where all further actions and choices moved me toward the day when I would be forced to flee my home and give up my music, it would be the time I put my flute on the bench outside my house when my mother demanded I take bread and cheese to my father working in his fields. So much of my childhood was taken up with ways to get out of my chores that should anyone from my childhood see me now, they might not believe it was me. I've grown some, yes, but I also no longer have the music to fill my time. And as music filled so much of my time, I tried to be away from my flute as little as possible, but I also took steps to protect it and ensure its safety. Accidents happen, and when the other children in the town dislike you because you have a gift they do not, and your lazy habits are tolerated a bit more because of that gift, sometimes what seems like an accident isn't. That day, I had chosen to leave my flute on the bench rather than argue with my mother about taking it back to my room. Arguing would have kept me from it longer than it would take to run to my father in the field and back, and run I did, as fast as my legs would move me. Because of trouble I'd gotten into over the years with other village children, I'd learned to put on quite the burst of speed when needed.

Now, if I'd put the flute down on one of the chairs behind the house, or taken the time to argue with my mother, things might have been different. If, after everything, I had the chance to go back and make another choice, would I have? I cannot tell. Most likely not, but I say that with the comfort of not actually having that choice to make.

When I returned home, my flute was not on the bench where I had left it. I glanced around frantically, hoping that it had only rolled off. It wasn't anywhere I could see it. I drew in a deep lungful of air to call to my mother – please, gods and goddesses, let her have taken it inside – when I heard someone cough loudly in the street behind me, the very directed cough of someone trying to get my attention.

I turned and saw Hugh, Eric, and Gregory smiling at me. Those triplets had caused the greater portion of the unhappy moments in my childhood. Hugh stood in the middle, slightly taller than the other two, all three of them easily a head higher than me or any other boy or girl in the town. In that place, in that time, childhood lasted much longer than here, where girls look to marry at fifteen or sixteen. Girls in my hometown were still sometimes playing with dolls, and boys were not yet given the responsibilities in the fields and town reserved for grown men, and most of them still played at being knights with wooden swords. Well, Hugh, the largest boy in the town, held my flute in one hand.

"Give. It. Back." I took a step forward to punctuate every word.

"No," Hugh said. "Your parents obviously don't love you enough to keep you honest about your chores, so we're going to."

I ground my teeth together. Even after all these years, I can still remember the ache in my jaw as I struggled to keep from screaming at him. Screaming would have brought adults, and that was cheating. By the unwritten, unspoken laws of the children in our town, if the adults got involved, you lost status in the eyes of everyone else. I had so little status that I couldn't afford to lose any. Also, if everyone found out what had set me off, and the three brutes looking at me with malicious grins would surely tell them, everyone would know what kind of a reaction stealing my flute would produce. Oh yes, anyone who caused another child to get an adult involved gained standing in the eyes of the other children. Needless to say, Hugh, Eric, and Gregory collectively held as much status in this game as all the other children put together.

"Whether or not I get my chores done has no effect on you three," I said.

"Oh, but it does," Eric said. "Any time any of the rest of us shirk our chores even the slightest bit, we get compared to you." He pitched his voice up an octave or two. "'Well now, since you don't mind your duties, let's get you a fiddle so you can run off and play with Elzibeth.'"

"Maybe if you didn't have a flute," Gregory said, "you'd be able to be a bit more like the rest of us."

My ears grew warm. I ground my teeth together even harder.

"May I please have my flute back?" I said through my teeth.

"Perhaps," Hugh said. He twirled the flute in his fingers. "But you have to do something first."

"What?" I asked, dreading the amount of work they were going to heap on me, or the embarrassing act they were going to make me perform, humiliating me before as many in the town as possible.

"Spend the night in the dragon's cave," they said in unison.

"Fine," I replied.

From the way their faces scrunched up in befuddlement, I'm sure they hadn't thought that I'd actually agree. I would worry my parents a bit, and surely

I'd see some form of punishment, but it wasn't nearly as bad as I feared. I spun on my toe, went into the house, and collected my cloak, some food, and one of my father's lanterns with several extra candles. Mother was so busy preparing the stew for dinner that she hardly noticed me. She said something about getting some chore done before getting back to playing my flute, but I hardly noticed her.

"I'll see you tomorrow," I said, pushing my way through the brothers.

I got about twenty or so paces beyond them, when I heard that attention-getting cough again. I stopped and glanced back.

"You have to bring proof," Hugh said.

I gave a sharp nod and left town.

II

Everyone knew generally where the dragon's cave was, but nobody went because it was in the wild hills north of the town. Also, the last man to go to the dragon's cave, in the time when my grandfather was a child, never returned. When people gathered at the tavern, every once in a time, someone would speak of that knight that went into the hills and never came back. People would speculate as to his fate, and even as to why he'd gone up there in the first place. No one had seen any sign of a dragon in more years than anyone could guess at. And even without fear of dragons that probably weren't there anyway, the wild hills contained more than enough real dangers: wild boars, wolves, and the occasional sinkhole. Natives of small towns generally share one common trait, and I've seen many small towns. People who live in them tend to have enough sense not to go looking after trouble.

I scrambled through the hills and crags and brambles for hours. I'd narrowly avoided a wild boar and soaked myself up to the waist by not being able to quite jump across a stream. Scrapes and cuts covered my hands, and I had a large lump on my head from failing to climb the edge of a ravine. Apparently, I didn't have enough sense not to go looking for trouble. Well, in my defense, I hadn't gone looking for three bullies to force me into this. Yes, I could have gone to my parents, but such thinking was impossible in the pride of my youth.

The sun had set, and the shadows between the hills had grown long enough and deep enough that I'd lit the first candle in the lantern. I'd come to the area where people said the dragon cave might be, and I'd been wandering back and forth, searching for it. I was about to give up for the night and find a place to sleep when I found it. I came around a hill, and there it was, a black opening in the side of the largest hill I could see. I'd come here planning to climb to the top and use it as a vantage point.

Now I didn't know if this really was the dragon's cave, but I couldn't imagine it being anything else. In my mind, I'd known that there was a dragon cave. I'd known it was in the wild hills. I just wasn't prepared for the enormity of it. It was somewhere between fifty and sixty paces away from me, and I could tell the top of the cave was at least ten times as high as I was tall. It hung in the side of the hill, dark and gaping, like some mouth waiting to swallow an unsuspecting passerby. Thinking that did nothing to settle my growing nerves, and I froze there, staring at it.

I might have stayed there all night, unmoving, but a wolf howled somewhere in the distance. That got my feet moving again. While a dragon might be waiting somewhere in the bowels of that cave, the cave might also be empty. On the other side of the coin, the wolves were very much real. The dragon, even if it was there, might not devour me whole, but I thought I'd probably prefer getting eaten in one gulp by a dragon than I would getting ripped apart by a pack of wolves. I hurried toward the cave, thinking that if a dragon had ever lived there at any time in the past, wolves and other wild animals would probably stay away from it. Quick death or a safe place, the cave seemed the wisest choice.

Even with all my logic and sound reasoning, stepping across the threshold of that cave was the hardest thing I've ever done in my life. As I write these words, my heart pounds at the memory. My stomach nearly emptied itself of the cheese and bread I'd eaten hours before.

The light of the lantern went before me a few paces and then faded into a gloomy haze. The air in the cave felt heavy, as if pressing down on me and stamping out my light. Still fearing the wolves more than any potential nastiness I might find in the cave, I went further inside.

A gust of wind caused the candle light to flutter a bit, and I thought I saw something move across the floor to my left. I nearly dropped the lantern and ran screaming from the cave. As it was, I gave a squeak of surprise but managed to stay in place. I held my breath and tried willing my heart to slow as I waited for the light to steady. When the wind died down and the candle ceased flickering, I realized it was my own shadow. I had the lantern in my right hand, and my shadow stretched out into the darkness. It weaved and danced every time I moved the lantern a bit. I released my held breath in a long, steady exhale.

It was still light enough to see outside, so I placed the lantern on the floor of the cave and went to gather firewood. This area didn't have as many trees as some parts of the hill I'd been through, but I'd noticed more than a few branches that would make a nice fire and more than enough twigs for kindling. In only a few minutes, I had enough wood to build and feed a nice fire to keep me warm until I was ready for sleep. A few minutes after that, and thanks to the candle in the lantern, I had a fire burning fifteen paces into the cave.

The light of the fire fared much better at pushing back the darkness than my little lantern. Placing another small piece of wood on the fire, I stood up, stretched, and looked around.

And screamed.

III

Even before my mind realized I should be scared, I screamed. I distinctly recall wondering exactly what it was I was screaming about. The scream was definitely my scared scream, which was very different from my angry scream or my sad scream. The fear scream is my highest pitch scream, hurting even my own ears.

Then my mind realized what I was screaming about. It had been too much for my rational thoughts to process all at once.

Silhouetted against the wall, I saw the flickering shadow of a great, gaping maw filled with twin rows of giant teeth. I backed away, shaking my head at the impossibility that there really was a dragon living in the dragon's cave. Then again, if there hadn't been a dragon, that knight probably would have come back. But he didn't. Still backing away, I wondered what happened to the knight.

My voice caught in my throat when I saw what created the shadow on the wall. The flickering firelight revealed the stark, pale skull of what used to be a dragon. Its mouth gaped open wide enough to likely swallow me whole. The shortest of the teeth in that mouth were longer than my forearm. My gaze swept down its long neck until I could take in the sight of its ribs and wings, unfurled out across the roof of the cave. A lance, blackened and charred, stabbed between two of the skeletal ribs. A suit of armor, also black and standing in a scorched area ten paces across, held onto the other end of that lance.

I don't know how long I stood transfixed by the sight of the skeletons of the dragon and the roasted knight, trapped in a moment of mutual murder. Hours had passed. By the time I was able to pull my gaze away, the candle in my lantern had melted away and the fire had burned to embers. I think it was the night's cold that finally overcame my awe. Wrapping my cloak around me, I rebuilt the fire.

Sleep would be impossible. I knew that, so I left the cave to gather more firewood. In the distance, wolves howled in the night, but none of them sounded closer than the first howl that urged me into the cave. Even with the knight and the dragon long dead, I could hardly blame the wolves for wanting to stay away.

When I returned to the cave, I built the fire higher than I needed to. The warmth of it helped to settle my nerves. Every few minutes I turned to warm another part of my body. I'd thought facing toward the skeleton and armor would be bad, looking on them as my back soaked in heat. Not so. Facing toward the fire was the worst. As my back cooled, it reminded me that a massive battle had taken place behind me, one where both combatants had died. Staring into the flames, my imagination glanced over my shoulder from time to time and saw the heads of both the dragon and the knight twisting silently to look upon me, as if asking, "Who is this interloper that disturbs us?" Shortly after that, my actual head would whip around to make sure they weren't stalking toward me. Granted, the thought that a suit of armor and a massive jumble of bones might make a little noise while trying to creep up on me had not occurred to me.

Eventually I nodded off to sleep. I didn't want to. I fought it as hard as I could, pinching myself and slapping my face. It didn't matter what I did, what I tried. The journey to the cave had taxed my body, and what I discovered there had taxed my mind. Both needed time to recuperate. I remember telling myself I would only rest my eyes for a moment. That a moment was all I'd need to be rested again. My eyelids came together. It felt so nice, as if closing my eyes had given my body permission to relax. The fire was so warm. Sleep came moments later.

When I woke, the fire was nothing but ashes and the sun had been up for a few hours at least. I stretched, trying to release some of the stiffness I'd gotten sleeping on the hard rock of the cave's surface. My back popped twice, and I let out a soft groan. Then my mind caught up with my situation, and the realization of where I was hit me as the last of the fog of sleep lifted from me.

I was on my feet at once, heart pounding in my chest, breath coming in short blasts.

Neither of them had moved. I don't know why that surprised me, but the part of me that imagined them turning and looking at me expected them to have gotten a little closer, maybe a lot closer. The mind and imagination play strange tricks on us when covered by the wet cloak of fear. In the months to come, I'd learn that lesson again and again, through pain and tears.

But, I'm getting ahead of myself.

The daylight helped me to calm down sooner than the night before, to get past the momentary fear that came over me, especially with the realization that I'd done it. I'd spent the night in the dragon's cave. I could get my flute back. Then I remembered that Hugh had said I needed to bring back proof.

What could I take that I'd be able to carry all the way back to the town?

I looked around. There had to be something. Perhaps one of the scorched rocks next to the knight? No. They'd be able to say I'd just burned a rock in a fire. Maybe I could find an old scale or something, so I searched behind the scattered rocks and in the corners of the cave. When I came to the very back of the cave, where the daylight barely reached, I saw three large rocks. They came up to about my waist, and each was smooth as polished glass. One was red as any ruby. One was green as any emerald. One was blue as any sapphire. These must be all that was left of the dragon's hoard. They would be the perfect proof, but I couldn't imagine rolling one all the way back to town.

With a huff and a stamp of my foot, I turned away from those stones that must have been worth the ransom of a kingdom. The dragon loomed above me. I followed the curve of its body from its head to its tail and down to its toes. Then I saw my proof. I could take the smallest of its toe bones. It would be easy to carry, probably no heavier than a shovel or other farm tool. My shoulders might ache by the time I returned to town, but I'd get my flute back.

Slowly, I worked my way toward the dragon's forward-most foot. It was the left one. The right was braced up against the wall. The hind feet supported most of the dragon's weight.

Then I stopped.

I'd seen skeletons before, deer and other animals in the woods south and west of town and sometimes livestock that had died alone in one of the further fields. None of them had ever held their shape. Each and every one had come apart as the muscles and sinew rotted away.

How then, in all the years since my grandfather's childhood, had this dragon managed to not tumble to the floor?

"Because it's a dragon," I told myself, and that settled it. I needed no other explanation or rationalization.

With that pronouncement, I started toward the foot again. My progress was slow and careful. The thing might remain whole because of whatever lingering magic it had possessed as a dragon, but that did not mean it would stay that way forever. When I was two paces away, I began to hold my breath. I reached down to the smallest of the toe bones, and biting my lips, I took a slow deep breath through my nose to steady my quivering hand. Holding my breath was apt to make me more tense and shaky than not. I closed my eyes and swallowed, despite the dryness that had filled my mouth. My imagination saw the whole thing coming down on me, bones tumbling in a great cacophony that would drown out my scream. Dust settling over my cairn, with no one to mourn me.

I pushed that thought out of my mind, reached out, and snatched up the toe bone.

My breath caught in my throat as a great creaking sound echoed in the cave. My feet wanted to flee, but I forced myself to stand fast. Any further disturbance in the cave might bring the thing down. I waited, not breathing, counting my heartbeats. Ten, the creaking stopped.

Twenty, the last echo of the creaking faded. Thirty, silence. Forty, I began to leave the cave, making sure I brought my feet completely off the floor and placing them carefully back down with hardly any jarring and definitely no shuffling.

I didn't take my first full breath until after I had left the cave completely. After my third breath, I laughed and laughed, skipping my way back toward home. I cradled the bone, which honestly wasn't much bigger than my flute, under my arm.

When I came to the place where I would turn out of sight of the cave, I turned back. In the full light of morning, the cave did not look as ominous as it had the night before. It was still huge, still like a gaping mouth, but it no longer held me in the grip of near-terror. I spun the toe bone in my hand and gave a rakish bow a boy might do to an adult's back after having danced out of some bit of serious trouble.

The Dragon Bone Flute

IV

The journey back to town took longer than the journey the day before. Yesterday, I had the passion of my anger to fuel my speed, and I wasn't carrying the extra load of the toe bone. I also had food and water. In my haste to escape the cave, I'd left the basket and what remained of my food behind. My water skin had been in the basket, too. I found plenty of streams to drink from, but my stomach growled with hunger. Despite this, I was also filled with a sense of wonder and awe, seeing the world in a new light. Now that I knew the truth of the dragon's cave, I saw many signs that it had once lived here: a small valley between two hills filled with the sun-bleached bones of what looked like several hundred cows, a grove of burned down trees where no other plants grew, and several places where I imagined I could see the dragon's tracks. This last one was pure foolishness. In all the decades since the dragon and knight had killed each other, the weather would have washed away any fleeting sign of the dragon's passing. On the other side of the coin, the dragon's skeleton had remained together. Who knew what else was possible?

By the time I returned to town late in the afternoon, my feet hurt worse than any time in my whole life. The fog of wonder had lifted. I just wanted to get my flute back, play a few songs, and go to sleep in my own bed. I'd probably receive a stern talking to from my parents. Mother might even yell, and I could live with that. I hoped my father didn't get too quiet. The quieter he grew, the worse it was, especially when he gave me his most I'm-disappointed-in-you look. It always wrenched my insides so much that my stomach and heart seemed to trade places. But mostly, I just wanted to get my flute back.

Hugh, Eric, and Gregory stood in the middle of the road back into town. I adjusted my path a bit and headed right toward them.

Gregory, or perhaps it was Eric – I couldn't tell because I was so tired and fixated on the flute in Hugh's hand – said something. His brothers laughed.

"Did you get to the cave?" Hugh asked, still chuckling a bit.

"Yes." I shoved the toe bone at him. "Here's your proof. Give me my flute back."

They all looked at the bone for a moment, eyes wide with wonder for just a moment. Then Eric laughed and pointed.

"You're trying to convince us that deer bone is your proof?"

"It is," I said. "The dragon is dead. That's a bone from its toe. It's the only one small enough for me to carry."

The other two brothers took up his laughter.

"The only thing you've proven is that you're a liar," Hugh said. "And liars need to be punished."

Before I could do or say anything else, Hugh grasped my flute with one hand on either end and brought it down across his knee. The sound of my flute snapping would haunt me longer than I could imagine. I fell to my knees as the splintered halves of my prized possession fell to the ground.

I grasped one piece in each hand and looked up at the three bullies. In my youth, in my hometown, I hardly knew what that term meant. Sure, my parents used it when describing the tax collector who came once a year, complaining about how he'd bully people around. I didn't understand what it really meant until after I'd traveled far and wide, so that when I call the brothers bullies, I'm speaking in terms I know now, not from any level of comprehension as it happened. They were bullies of the worst sort, because as I knelt in the road, blinking tears of sorrow and loss out of my eyes, I heard gasps from all around. I found out later that the brothers had told all of the other children where I'd gone and what I was supposed to do. Hugh had not destroyed my flute to punish me. He'd done it to solidify his fearful reign over the other children of the town. That much I understood. Even in my stunned state, I knew it hadn't mattered what I had brought back. He and his brothers had decided I was going to be their example, their object lesson. Well they, too, could serve as an example. I was not about to be made a fool of, nor was I going to let them get away with this.

Hugh reached out and placed a hand on my shoulder. His touch was light, almost like a caress.

"Let's get you home," he said in a tone that must have been what he thought of as caring but only came out sounding spiteful. "Your parents must be worried about you."

I met his eyes. I could see myself reflected in them. The dust of the road clung to my tear-stained face in dark-brown strips. When I smiled at Hugh, my lips thin and pressed together, he blinked a few times. I'm sure that wasn't the reaction he'd expected.

I'm also sure he wasn't expecting me to stab him in the hand with one of the jagged ends of my ruined flute, but I did. Hard. Blood welled from over a dozen wounds in a tight circle. Several of them were rather deep. I twisted my makeshift weapon, hoping to give him splinters.

I tried to get him in the leg with the other half of the flute, but by that time the surprise had worn off Hugh and his brothers. Eric and Gregory grabbed my arms and twisted them behind me. I struggled for a second, but that only made them wrench my arms harder.

Fighting only made it hurt more, but not as much as it did when Hugh slapped me.

I'd been slapped before, but nothing like this. This was no angry child slap. He put his whole body into it. Pinpoints of light and dark circles filled my vision. My jaw ached, and my skin burned. I remember thinking it a miracle that he didn't rattle any of my teeth loose.

Not knowing, or not wanting to leave well enough alone, I kicked Hugh in the shin, then stomped on one of his brother's, Eric's I think, feet. Unfortunately, it wasn't enough to make Eric let go of me, and my kick to Hugh only made him angrier. He balled his hand into a fist and drove it into my stomach. I coughed all the air out of my lungs.

At that point, I was in so much pain and so exhausted from my journey to the dragon's cave that my mind began to shut the world out. I was vaguely aware of other people yelling and the sound of feet stomping. There was more yelling. Someone picked me up and was carrying me somewhere. At some point, I was placed onto something soft and someone put some blankets over me.

I slept.

V

It's been years since I thought of that night, but even now, I can feel the sweat prickling through my pores from the fitful dreams I had. I don't recall the events of those dreams in any semblance of coherence, just images: broken flutes, splinters of wood raining down on me, maniacal laughter, and rivers of blood gushing from the dying bodies of Hugh, Gregory, and Eric. Please don't think me too morbid. I was in that place between childhood and adulthood, and my imagination was trying to balance between both those states of mind after having suffered the worst trauma of my life. Little did I know, it was just the beginning.

At some point in the night, I woke. It was a gibbous moon that night, and the light of it shown in through the window making everything shadowy lumps. I blinked in the darkness of my room. The pain from where Hugh had slapped my face and struck my stomach was now a dull ache. The burning my cheek had felt was almost gone, and I thought the slight throbbing in my jaw would last the longest of all of them. Thankfully Hugh wasn't much more than a boy, yes a large one, but not at the point where he really knew anything about fighting. The townsfolk weren't violent by nature, but sometimes the young, mostly unmarried, men got drunk at the tavern and settled their drunken ramblings with fists. I sat up, irritated that I was awake, but also thankful to be away from the dreams.

Then I heard a tapping somewhere. Three taps. Silence. Three taps. Silence. I looked around, still trying to blink away the haze of sleep and bad dreams. After a few moments, I stopped trying to see it, closed my eyes, and just listened. The sound was coming from my window.

I crawled out from under my blankets. The night chill hit me, and I shivered as I crossed the room. When I reached the window, I saw the moon first, hanging in the center of the frame. That meant I'd only been asleep a few hours, just long enough to sleep off the shock and initial heartache of my loss. I saw the silhouette of a head in the window – too short to be an adult, not that an adult would be at my window at this hour, but also not tall enough to be one of the brothers.

For a few moments I pondered whether or not to open the window. I was fairly certain I knew who it was, and I wasn't sure I wanted to deal with him. Unfortunately, he would probably keep tapping away at the window until I opened it and dealt with him.

"Hello, Frances," I said as I opened the window.

A blast of cold air hit me as the wind gusted into my room, and I wrapped my arms around my shoulders. Even though my clothes offered a bit more warmth than my nightgown would have, my shivering increased.

"Elzibeth," he said through chattering teeth, "I brought you these."

Frances was a boy of slight build, and though a year older than me, he was shorter by a few inches. He reached up toward the window, holding the two halves of my broken flute and the dragon's toe bone.

"I got them before anyone else could," Frances said. "I thought you might like them, but now I don't know. Maybe not. But if they're going to get thrown away, you should do it. After all, they're your things."

I took them.

"Thank you, Frances. Now go home."

I closed the window before he could say anything else and went back to my bed. Even curling up in the blankets, I couldn't sleep yet. The cold night air had chilled the sleep right out of me, at least for a while. Since sleep would be a little time off, I laid the things Frances had saved for me on the bed, right in the middle of a patch of moonlight. Looking at the remains of my flute, part of me wanted to start crying all over again, but for some reason the tears wouldn't come. Frances' kindness stopped them. At least someone in the village had cared enough about my feelings and what I might want to…well, I don't know, but he did something, made a gesture that helped to draw me away from complete despair.

My eyes wandered away from my ruined flute and looked over the dragon toe bone. It was broken as well. One end had been stepped on, or something like that, because while one end stopped in a smooth knob, the other end had become as jagged and splintered as the broken bits of my flute. I picked it up and turned it around in my hands. When the broken edge faced me, I stopped and lifted it up so I could get a better look.

The bone was free of marrow, as I expected. However, the part I didn't expect was how much empty space there was inside the bone, like a bird's. Growing up in a small community, I'd seen the insides of plenty of bones, and this discovery surprised me to say the least.

I chewed the inside of my cheek, because that's what I've done all my life whenever something intrigues or interests me.

For a long time, I sat with my blankets wrapped around my shoulders staring at the oddity, trying to figure out why exactly a dragon's bones would be hollow. Before I allowed sleep to take me, I went over to my wardrobe and got out my work knife. I used the knife to carve away the dragon bone's jagged edges. When it was mostly blunt, and I wouldn't have to worry about stabbing myself with the edges, I pushed the remains of my flute and bone under my pillow. For some reason, the lumps they made brought me a bit of comfort, as if proving that even in the worst moments, sometimes people still care. I'd have to remember to thank Frances a little more properly the next time I saw him.

VI

Two days later Frances's cheek flared a furious crimson in response to the kiss I'd planted on it. He'd come up to me, awkwardly asking how I was. While he was in the middle of his babbling, I leaned forward and kissed him. Nothing special, just a quick peck, but that was more intimacy than either of us had shared with another human being aside from our parents. Once I'd done it, his mouth opened and closed, trying to find words. Realizing what I'd done, I felt my cheeks begin to heat as well.

"Wha…wha…what?" he managed, at last.

"That was to thank you for bringing those things to me," I replied.

I couldn't say what he'd brought out loud, especially not the bone. In the two days since my fight with the brothers, two things had gotten around to all the other children. The first was that I'd not only stood up to the brothers but actually started a fight with them. The second was that I'd claimed to have found a dragon bone. This collective knowledge had been received with a bit of a mixed opinion. For now, the other children were overlooking the audacity of the dragon business due to

Hugh, Eric, and Gregory being much more closely watched by the adults in the town. Oh, of course their parents, especially their boisterous father, had made all sorts of justifications for them attacking me, mostly based on the gash on Hugh's hand. That didn't hold much weight when so many people had seen the two smaller boys holding me while Hugh looked ready to beat me senseless. The result was that they wouldn't be getting away with any of their bullying for quite some time.

"You're welcome," Frances said, and his blush deepened. I'm fairly certain mine did, too.

We stood looking at our feet. After a while, Frances broke the silence

"I need to get back," Frances said. "My da' has things for me to do."

I nodded. "Thank you again."

He nodded back. "Of course."

I watched him walk away, the frail, skinny boy who had done me the greatest kindness of my life to that point.

And that was the extent of our interaction for some time.

I moved from moment to moment in a strange sort of haze. I didn't have a flute anymore. I didn't have music anymore. I'd tried singing and whistling, and these two activities were poor substitutes for my grandfather's flute.

For me, playing the flute had been about more than just making music. It had been an activity that I put my whole self into. My mind had to remember the notes of the melody and make sure that I wasn't rushing or slowing down the tempo of my song. Where most musicians content themselves with the motions of making music with their fingers, more often than not, I would move my body in rhythm to my songs, giving the music physical form. Lastly, or maybe it was firstly, I poured my heart into every piece I did. I can't describe it any more than that, except to say that whenever I played a song, my mood at the time colored the tune, sometimes making the song unrecognizable.

My parents noticed my melancholy, and Father would frequently promise me, at dinner while I was pushing my uneaten food around on my plate, that he'd get me a new flute when a peddler came through the town. He meant well with these promises, but we never had extra money, especially when a peddler came.

After a few months of my moping and listening to Father's hollow promises, a peddler finally came to town. He arrived just between the last of the autumn rains and the first of the winter snows. I never understood how they could tell, but I suppose it's the business of peddlers to know these things, just as the blacksmith knows the right glow of yellow to start hammering a pot or the farrier knows exactly how much to trim to keep from hobbling a horse.

The peddler stayed a week.

When he left, I did not have a new flute.

Still, I didn't completely give up hope. We usually saw two or three peddlers before winter. The first snow came the next day. We wouldn't see another peddler until spring.

I did not come out of my room for three days. I did not speak to my father for nearly a month.

However, having foreseen this, I'd taken steps to keep myself occupied during the winter. I'd not been able to afford one of the three flutes the peddler had for sale, but he did have a small woodcarving kit that I traded for doing all his laundry during his stay. Before the snows grew too deep, I collected all manner of sticks, reeds, and branches. The time I'd spent playing in previous years I dedicated to woodworking. My hands blistered, bled, and calloused. I slept little, working at night by feel as I'd played by feel, as I'd closed my eyes and felt the music well inside me, burning and pushing to be free on the air. However, I didn't carve and whittle all the time. In those moments when I didn't, I held the bone, feeling it, studying it, knowing it with my hands.

VII

When the snows finally began to melt, I was ready. One morning, just after Father had gone to the fields, I made a bedroll, bundled my warmest clothes into a pack, and gathered a bit of food I thought would last a few days: dried meat and fruit, cheese, bread, a skin of small beer. The remains of Grandfather's flute were tucked away at the bottom of my pack, and the dragon bone was in the bedroll.

"What are you doing?" Mother asked as I came out of the pantry.

"Leaving for a few days," I replied.

She opened her mouth, but I held up my hand.

"I need music, Mother," I said. "You and I both know I'm never getting a flute from a peddler. I'm going to make my own, but I need to be completely alone. I have to go to a special place, where nothing will bother me, so I can get it perfect."

"The dragon cave." It wasn't a question.

I nodded and waited for her to forbid me.

Instead, she sighed. "Knowing you, you'll just run off the moment my back is turned, and won't even have the benefit of having food." She hugged me. "Your father is going to be furious."

I returned Mother's embrace. "Let him be. He'll recover by the time I return."

"We can hope," Mother said. She kissed me on the cheek. "Be as careful as you can."

"I will."

And before either of us could dissolve into tears, I left.

The air was brisk, swift and biting on my nose and cheeks. It was such a change from the warm autumn breeze the last time I'd made this journey. Townsfolk were about their chores and business, including many children. My clothes and pack made it obvious that I was going on some kind of journey.

Word spread ahead of me, as it does in every small town and village I've ever known.

By the time I reached the last house in the town proper, Hugh, Eric, and Gregory were there, waiting. I hadn't seen any of them in months. They'd grown over the winter and had developed a bit of facial hair, though not enough to make them look like men. Rather, with their feet spread wide and fists on their hips, they looked like boys attempting to play at being men.

The brothers mocked me, trying to get a rise out of me. Their words had no effect. What were words compared to the last pains they'd given me. I paid them no mind as I walked north past the last house in the town proper.

Getting to the dragon cave took the whole of daylight. In the hills, snow still clung to the earth in patches here and there, especially in the valleys and ravines where I'd normally travel. The land where the snow had melted away was slick and muddy. Only the few places where large rocks pierced the earth offered sure footing, and I came to treasure these rare moments of easy travel.

Shadows stretched over everything by the time the cave loomed above me. The air turned even colder, made worse by the wind that came as the sun sank behind the horizon. I hurried to start a fire, cursing myself for forgetting a lantern. My fingers shook, not only from cold, but also with a bit of fear. Again, I felt the huge skeleton and the charred armor turning to look at me as I struck flint against steel.

At last, I got the fire going, despite my unsteady fingers and the mostly wet wood I'd gathered. I built it large and warm and laid my blankets out to soak up the heat. Oddly, once the fire lit the cave, I didn't feel as if I was being watched by that same, ever-present stare. I looked around for signs that any animals might be using this cave as shelter in the winter, and found no evidence of this, not even bat droppings. In any other instance, I might be surprised, but not here. For a time, I looked out into the night, listening to the wolves howling to each other and to the owls with their haunting calls. These two would have normally scared me beyond sleep, but I knew they would not bother me here. Glancing back at the skeleton, I did not blame them. Eventually, as the fire burned low, I rolled up in my blankets, put my head on my pack, and drifted to sleep.

The next morning, I broke my fast on cheese, dried fruit, and bread. I melted a bit of snow in my metal cup for something to drink. I couldn't stand small beer in the morning, and unfortunately I'd forgotten tea. So much forgotten when I'd believed I'd planned so well. On the other side of the coin, my mind had been on other things, well, one other thing – the task I'd set for myself and the reason I'd returned to this place.

After I finished eating, I laid out my woodworking tools.

I'd gathered quite a collection of knives, drills, hooks, and chisels. When I'd taken this up at the beginning of winter, Father had gone about the town, trading small casks of his plum ale for tools. I suppose it was his way of attempting to bridge the gap that had grown between us.

With my tools laid out, I took the dragon's toe bone into my hands and closed my eyes. I let my fingers wander over it as I had all winter. I knew the touch of it, every inch, all the tiny nicks that covered its surface. Even with

42

this familiarity, I needed to know it better. I felt I had one chance at my plan. If I failed, I don't believe I'd have had the heart to try again. So I studied the bone for that entire first day. I did reach for my tools a few times. Each time, I left them be. I was not in any rush. True, I might eventually get hungry, but that didn't concern me much. My task would be completed or failed long before true hunger became a danger to me.

The next day I took my tools to the bone. It took me the better part of the day to remove the knob from the other end of the bone and smooth out both edges.

I suppose I could go into every detail of how I carved and whittled my new flute. It was the greatest thing I've ever done, and now that I'm writing of it, each moment of the task becomes crisp and clear in my mind. Even after all these years, I believe I could do it again. But I will not tire you with every little cut and slice. Four days later, I finished the flute midmorning. Well, I'd finished cutting and carving. I did not know if I'd actually completed the task I set for myself.

Three and a half days of work rested on my palms. I'd been so careful, sometimes taking hours just to decide how much or how little to shave off the edge of a finger hole. Now I had to test it. I've never been so afraid of anything in all my life.

Timidly, as if I were leaning in to actually kiss Frances on the cheek, I brought the dragon bone flute to my lips. I inhaled deeply through my nose, held it in my lungs for a few moments, and then blew out through pursed lips.

The sound that filled the cave was the most perfect note I'd ever made, ever heard from a flute or any other instrument. My heart sang, and I forgave my father. If he had gotten me a poor peddler's flute, I'd have never heard this note, let alone have been responsible for creating the instrument that sounded it.

However, one tone does not an instrument make. I placed my fingers above the holes. The true test would be to play an entire song. I let my breath slide across the flute and began to play.

The flute did not create music. It created bliss. The sound that came from it was purer and truer than anything I'd ever heard. Though my breath and fingers went through the familiar motions of the songs I knew, the flute seemed to make them solid in some strange way, as if this flute were playing the first music the world had ever really known. I wish that I were a poet so that I could truly explain what it was like in the cave, creating such beauty. I am not, so I'll cease trying to convince you to understand something that cannot be grasped by the mind, only felt deep down in the places where one knows the love of a husband or wife or mother or father.

I played for hours. When I exhausted all the songs I knew, I improvised, having done it often enough wandering around the town, skipping my feet to whatever melody came from my heart. In that moment, I played a mixed melody of sorrow and wonder. Sorrow at the loss of my grandfather's flute, and wonder at the treasure I'd created. With my eyes closed, I played and played. As tears rolled down my cheeks, I played and played.

Finally, hours later – perhaps days, for I had no knowledge or caring of time with the flute at my lips – I finished. I'd played all the sorrow and loss out of my heart. The flute left my lips, and I sat in the quiet. In the wake of my song, the whole world seemed a bit quieter than before, still, as if everything around, even the stones, were afraid to move because the song might start up again.

I stood up and walked up to where the dragon and knight were frozen in time, forever killing each other. I glanced at the place where the toe bone had been before I'd taken it so many months before. Had it only been months? It seemed so much longer than that, felt like I'd gone through so many changes.

Holding the flute up to the skeleton, I said, "Thank you for this gift. I know I took a part of you away, and I apologize, but please know that I will treasure this always, and a part of you will help me bring a bit of magic back into the world.

"I thank you as well," a voice boomed in the cavern. I screamed. Long, loud, shrill, I screamed.

VIII

Some have called me a prideful woman, and they would be within their rights. Considering some of the things I've done and seen, I believe I am justified in that pride. My confidence suffers not a bit when I admit that I screamed like a small child being set upon by rabid hounds, such was my fear.

Part of my fear came from that booming voice, but only a part.

The rest came from the shimmering form that had surrounded the dragon's skeleton. It was silvery-white and appeared as if it might be the dragon's true form, or at least what it had been in life. I couldn't make out the details, as the shimmering wavered, showing nearly solid form one moment and almost completely transparent the next.

The one thing I could see was the eyes. They were bright, glowing orbs that remained solid, or at least looked solid, and they shone with an intellect older and wiser than I could possibly know. They seemed so human and so alien at the same time.

The shimmering head looked down on me, the way I'd imagined it had when I'd been sitting by the fire. My scream caught in my throat because my breath stopped. It seemed as if some primal reflex told me that if I didn't move, I might be safe, it might not notice me. So I didn't move. Not a bit.

"You have brought me joy that I thought I would never know again," the voice rumbled. "Again, you have my thanks."

So many desires battled against each other in my breast that day. I wanted to speak, to say something, anything, to this creature addressing me. I wanted to flee, but my feet seemed rooted to the floor. I wanted to beg for my life. No amount of thought would overpower that deep need to stay still, that basic understanding my body had that to stay still was to live.

After a few moments — it was waiting for me to respond, I suppose — it began to chuckle. The sound of it wrapped around me like an embrace, calming my fear with a gentle caress of amusement.

"Fear not, little one," the ghostly wyrm said, then chuckled again. "Apologies. Listen to me, the ghost of a dragon, telling you, the human child, not to be afraid. As if the mere telling of it will make it reality, as if my words hang with the truth of music. I might as well command the seasons to reverse."

Strange as it might seem, however, the dragon's voice did soothe me a bit, at least enough so that I felt the tension leave my muscles. I managed a curtsy, and with that familiar movement, my manners returned.

"I was not so much frightened," I said, "as I was startled, sir."

"Madam," the dragon replied.

"I'm sorry?" I asked.

"If you are going to give me a human, gender-based honorific," the dragon said, "then it would be madam, not sir. In life I was female."

"Oh, well then, it is my turn to apologize," I said.

"With the gift of music that you brought me, I have no choice but to accept and forgive you. What is your name?"

"Elzibeth."

"Well then, Elzibeth, give me one more song before you go. I believe your task is complete, and I recall that humans are social creatures."

I took a deep breath. For a moment I'd actually forgotten the town, the people, and my family. They'd faded from my mind in the face of this wonderful creature speaking to me. I knew I'd have to go back. As much as I desired a life of sitting here, playing my new flute, hearing what stories this dragon might have to tell, I knew it was not to be. Home was calling, and I couldn't ignore it forever.

So I put my flute up to my lips and played for the dragon who had given me this most wonderful thing in the world. I didn't play any of the songs I knew. I played of what the flute meant to me: life, joy, and freedom. Sitting here, putting these memories to paper, I'm left empty as I try to describe these things, again wishing I'd been born with the gifts of a poet. Just know that I filled the cave with a wonder and beauty that day that few humans had ever heard, such that when I stopped playing, the feeling of the music lingered a bit, like an echo but solid, giving weight to the air. Then, even that faded, as if carried away on a breeze.

The Dragon spoke no more. With nothing else to be done, I gathered my things and began the journey back to town.

IX

Night had fallen by the time I finally walked between the houses. It was a quiet night, as most were. Light from candles and lamps shone through the windows of some houses, but not all. We were not a raucous people, but it was spring, and the snows had melted, so many would be stretching stiff legs and backs as they began to prepare for the planting. Most people also gathered in the tavern, reacquainting themselves with their neighbors from across town and those that lived farther afield. A walk that normally took half an hour the rest of the year could take several hours during the winter, depending on the snow, so most people stayed at home during the winter.

As I came upon the tavern, I heard bits of conversation and laughter floating into the night's air. I sat on the steps and listened. Some people spoke of farming and what livestock they'd lost over the winter, while others gossiped about budding romances. I found myself wondering how soon I would be included in that circle, and surprisingly, I turned a few thoughts to Frances and how the winter had treated him. Then, I heard what I'd been waiting for, and all other thoughts vanished.

Hugh's deep, mocking laughter rolled out of the tavern. The sound of it made my skin crawl.

I entered the tavern, shutting the door a little more firmly than I needed to. People nearest the door turned their heads to see who had come in. Their conversations stopped when they recognized me. This quiet spread through the tavern as I walked between the tables to the huge fireplace. It wasn't the first time I'd made my way to that centerpiece of cobbled stones and mortar. We didn't have many minstrels who came to us, one, perhaps two a year at most, but a few townsfolk knew their way around an instrument and could manage to keep a melody with their voice, or understood how to tell a grand tale. When these people wanted to perform, they went to the fireplace, and tradition dictated everyone else give them attention. In return, the performer would not take up the whole evening, giving one to three performances at most. I'd first performed here in my seventh summer, sitting on my grandfather's knee.

When I reached the fireplace, I turned and looked directly at Hugh, Eric, and Gregory. All winter, as I whittled and carved, as my hands blistered and bled, I'd imagined all the terrible things I'd do to them, ways I'd get revenge for them breaking my flute. In that moment, when I saw them staring at me with narrowed eyes and tight mouths, I realized that this was the worst thing I could do. This was the perfect revenge, because they'd played their hand too strong last fall. They'd bullied me to the point of getting adults involved and so broken the children's law, so now the other children saw it as fair and right to get adults should those three get out of hand again. I'd known that from the few conversations I'd had over the winter. This meant I was relatively safe. It also meant my new flute was safe, well, as safe as could be with those three.

The flute came to my lips, and I began to play. "Skipping Through the Meadow" seemed a good first choice. It was a light, airy tune that went with a children's circle dance. More to the point, it was simple. Even as I sounded the first notes, trickles of sweat began to crawl down the back of my neck. It was warm by the fire, but not that warm.

Just like back at the cave, the music seemed to fill the empty spaces in the room, but not with a weight that pressed down. This time, the music seemed to lift people up. I played with my eyes open, mostly to avoid anything the three brothers might throw from the back of the room, but my attention did not remain on them. I saw people sitting up straighter, weaving a bit from side to side in time to the song. Some people started clapping along. More joined them. I had to play louder to be heard over the clapping, stamping, and pounding on tables. Geoffry, the tavern owner, and his wife, Gayle, moved through the common room, nearly skipping, grinning like this was their first night of business.

Somewhere in the middle, I stopped playing "Skipping Through the Meadow." The song didn't end. I kept playing, fingers dancing over the holes. But as I played, the spirit of the music became more important than the rigid structure of the song. The freedom and childlike wonder became the focus, and soon the music soared out on its own, as if skipping weren't enough anymore. The music took to the air and flitted over the meadow. Then that wasn't enough, and we who were caught in its wake were carried aloft to soar above the clouds. High notes and low intermingled, and I realized that this song must be what it was like for a dragon to fly, soaring and diving, weaving on the strange gusts of winds that must blast about high in the air.

Oh, sun, and moon, and stars, I'd forgotten how wonderful that sounded. Even now, I can hear my music in the back of my mind, how it seemed to take us all out of the tavern to where we could feel the wind on our faces. It's taking every bit of my will to remain here at the table, writing down my tale and not running off to make music again. I'm sure I remember how. But it's not the time for me to indulge myself.

As I played, the song took hold of me, and I became a mere vessel by which the music forced its way into our world. The song took on a harder edge as we flew from the skies down to the earth, toward a cave.

A few people in the tavern gasped as the notes grew deep and ominous. Smoke billowed into the common room in two nearly solid tendrils. One of these billowed into a dragon, wings unfurling as it soared above people's heads. The other became a knight strutting out of the fireplace with lance and shield.

The music clashed and so did the smoky visions of the dragon and the knight. They battled all through the common room. The crowd seemed to hold its breath as the music rose and fell in time with the ebb and flow of the fight taking place right about their heads. The knight and dragon spun and danced as the music carried them from one corner of the tavern to another. Finally, the knight managed to get inside the dragon's guard and thrust his lance into the dragon's breast, just as the dragon let fly a blast of smoky fire. The song came to a slow end as haunting low notes echoed and the smoke thinned.

I can't tell how long I played, but by the time the music ended, I was drenched with sweat. People stared back at me with strange expressions. Eyes were wide, and more than a few mouths hung open. In the near-silence that followed my performance, I heard feet shuffling under tables and one person coughed uncomfortably.

At this reaction, or maybe lack of reaction, I felt suddenly very alone and perhaps a little afraid. I had no idea how the townsfolk were going to respond to this sudden bit of magic, real magic and not some traveling performer's sleight-of-hand tricks, thrusting itself into their lives.

I got up and headed for the door, exiting as I'd entered, without a word, explanation, or apology. Eyes followed me. I did not look, but I'm sure the eyes that looked at me hardest, asking the most unspoken questions, belonged to Hugh, Eric, and Gregory.

When I finally reached the door, a journey that seemed even longer than the music I'd played, someone finally started clapping. I turned. Frances stood on a chair in the far corner of the room, slapping his hands together over and over again. Someone else started clapping over by the bar. It was my father. Others joined them, slowly at first, but then more and more. Voices added cheers and laughter to the rising din, and a few people pounded their mugs on tabletops.

I couldn't stop myself from grinning. I took a deep bow like I'd seen the minstrels and traveling performers do.

When I left the tavern, only three people weren't clapping.

After that, I went home. Mother embraced me and asked how I was, all the time checking over me as if doubting my word. I showed her my new flute. She asked me to play something for her. I played "Red Mountain Rose," a short piece, sweet and airy. Nothing strange happened; the fire remained the fire, and the song ended when I wanted it to end, though I must say, it sounded sweeter and crisper than any instrument I'd heard in all my days, before or since.

When I finished the song, Mother kissed both my cheeks. I hugged her and then went to my room, put my new flute under my pillow, and slept.

X

Over the next few months, I became quite the local celebrity. Rare was the night I was not at the tavern playing for at least a little while. Nothing happened like that first night; the smoke never came alive again. However, even without the extraordinary strangeness of my first performance, the townsfolk still loved the music I made with the flute. Well, all save for three, and the greater my small fame grew, the more those brothers glared at me from the back of the room or from behind everyone on the village green.

As time went on, Hugh, Eric, and Gregory grew grimmer and grimmer whenever we were forced to spend time together. They never did anything as blatantly hurtful as that day when they broke my flute, but they did seem to bump into me a bit more than anyone else, and while they were always quick to apologize, it seemed that I staggered from those chance encounters more and more frequently as time went on and my slight reputation grew. I took this all in stride. They weren't really hurting me, and I made sure to avoid being close to them, especially those times when we might be completely alone.

Time passed. Planting came and went with nothing out of the ordinary. Summer gave way to autumn and harvest, which then went into winter. People got hurt, but no more than usual and in no extraordinary ways. Animals died. Babies were born. The only thing that really changed was my playing, and that took the better part of a year for me to notice. Over time, I'd stopped playing the regular songs I knew, and more and more I took to playing about emotions or the feelings that come with a particular event.

One evening, late in the harvest, the tavern was quiet. Normally, end of harvest was a joyous and boisterous time, and that year should have been more so. It was the most successful harvest in memory. But despite that, Hugh, Eric, and Gregory's father had died. While their father had been working in the fields, a snake had startled his horse. The horse panicked, and while kicking about trying to get away from the snake and get free of the plow, it had kicked their father in the head. He'd most likely been dead before he'd even begun falling.

As was tradition, we held a wake for him in the tavern, body laid out on a white sheet, the one he'd be buried in. I didn't even really feel like being there. Mother and Father had made me go to show my respects to a member of the town passing, regardless of my personal feelings toward his sons. He'd never done me harm nor wrong, and they were right. So I took my flute, paid my respects, and then went and played quietly in the corner, not really close to the fire, because I didn't want to take the attention from the wake at that time. Songs and stories would come later, but not yet. Now was the time for quietly honoring his passage. I'd just planned to have a bit of soothing music just at the edge of things as people spoke their final words to the dead.

Eric came over to me. I stopped playing. A slight tension ran through the tavern. I noticed that Hugh and Gregory tensed more than anyone else, each glancing at the other with questioning eyes. Hugh shrugged, which I took to mean this wasn't some planned piece of taunting or humiliation they'd set up in order to feel better at my expense. That made me relax a bit, not completely, but a bit. When Eric stood in front of me, he couldn't quite meet my eyes.

"Could you," he said just above a whisper, "play something for my da'? Maybe something to ease him into his rest?"

I nodded, put my flute to my lips.

My song began as a lullaby. Soft notes flowed through the tavern. Soon though, the tone of the song shifted. I played of the balance between the seasons and between life and death. The lullaby transitioned into Spring, new life creeping into the world. Summer, full of fire and adventure, filled the tavern with deep, sharp tones that embraced its heady heat. As the heat settled into the crisp crackling notes of drying leaves and aching bones, Autumn took Summer's place. Winter came in after, cold and haunting, a mix of crisp high notes of the biting winds and the low, drawn sounds of endless white blanketing everything. As Winter seemed to end the song, just as after months of seemingly endless snow and ice and cold threatens to end life, the light, airy breath of Spring filled the room. I ended the piece with a rolling set of notes showing that hope remains even in the darkest of the coldest winters, that just like the seasons, life and death are a cycle, a continuous journey.

The tavern remained quiet for a long while after that. Then, as people seemed to take heart in the coming of life, townsfolk began to see Hugh, Eric, and Gregory not as their father's sons, but rather as the continuation of their father. People bought them drinks and congratulated them on the fine qualities each of them had received from their father. It became a joyous occasion, a celebration, and Hugh, Eric, and Gregory were at the heart of it.

Late in the night, when most people there were well into their cups, Hugh grabbed my shoulder and spun me around.

"My father loved dancing," Hugh said. "Play us something to dance to."

Cheers of agreement roared through the common room. Tables were moved aside, clearing a wide space in the center of the tavern. Men, young and old alike, scrambled to ask ladies to dance. As people took places and faced their partners, I began the first traditional song I'd played in months, a happy country dance. Those not dancing clapped along and laughed as too-drunk dancers stumbled through the movements.

One dance turned into another, and then another. People laughed and stumbled and jeered at each other. From my vantage point away from the dancers, I saw more than a few bottoms getting pinched – and not just ladies' bottoms.

During the fourth song, the tavern door burst open, crashing against one of the tables that had been pushed back. This startled me out of my playing. Someone shrieked in surprise.

Frances stood in the doorway, pointing up to the sky. Even in the candle and lantern light, it was easy to see the color had drained from his face.

"Dragon," he said. "In the sky. Dragon. Against the moon."

The Dragon Bone Flute

XI

Everyone rushed out of the tavern, including myself. People were talking, and I listened to snippets of their conversation.

"Really? A dragon?"

"How amazing."

"…probably a bat."

"…protect the livestock from…"

"…boy is daft…"

But they all went to see. At first no one saw anything. Then, a figure flew past the bright, blue-white orb of the moon. A long sinuous body, with wings that stretched and flapped, hung for a moment, illuminated in the sky. A few heartbeats later, it dove into the darkness of night. Gasps and cries of astonishment filled the air as I fled the town.

After I'd run for about half an hour, I began to realize what a poor choice I'd made, but I was young, foolish, and prideful. Once I'd set upon the journey, I refused to go back. Besides, someone might stop me. Still, even with the bright moon, once I got beyond the familiar herd paths, I seemed to find every hole and crack in the ground.

My grandfather used to say, "Desperation breeds creativity." After the third or fourth time I tripped, I realized that if I wanted to make it to the dragon cave without twisting or spraining an ankle, I needed to try something different. Well, I had myself and my flute. Three times I'd done something beyond explanation by playing my flute, each time with a different effect. Each time it was without intention. Who was to say that I couldn't direct an effect from whatever power the flute had?

So, I began to play. My song was light and airy, fleeting and quick, the perfect tune to make a journey seem shorter. I skipped and danced along with the tune, feet missing each and every dip and crack that might have tripped me. A wind picked up, always at my back, and it seemed to help speed me along.

As the early light of predawn crept into the eastern sky, I danced around a hill to see the dragon's cave gaping open before me. I stopped playing. When the music faded, so did the energy it gave me to keep moving. Exhaustion crashed down on me. My knees buckled, and I fell onto my backside amongst the dust and shrubs. I tried to get up but didn't have the strength. I tried to crawl toward the cave, but I only managed to sprawl into the dirt. My eyelids were heavy, closing despite my mind screaming at me that I needed to stay awake and get into the cave. My fatigue won over my will, and I fell into a deep, dreamless sleep.

Sometime later, I woke to someone shaking me. I blinked the dryness from my eyes, shook my head a bit to clear the sleep away, and looked to see Frances shaking me.

"Oh, thank the gods," he said.

"What are you doing here?" I asked, sitting up.

"When I saw you run out of the village, especially after we all saw the dragon flying around, I knew you were coming here," Frances said. "I thought..." His voice trailed off.

"Thought what?"

I stared him right in the face. He blushed and wouldn't meet my eyes. I snorted a brief laugh.

"You thought you were going to save the damsel from some nasty fate worse than death, didn't you?"

"No," Frances snapped at me. "I just worry. You're too reckless. One of these days you are going to get into trouble that you might not be able to get out of, trouble worse than Hugh, Eric, and Gregory."

I stood up and looked down at him. "Well, you might be right, but you aren't my keeper."

With that, I turned and headed toward the dragon's cave. I heard Frances scrambling to get up and follow me. He was sputtering something that might have been partway between an explanation and an apology, but I didn't pay him enough mind to really determine which.

He followed me into the cave, and promptly stopped talking. I glanced back at him. Frances stood looking at the skeletal dragon, mouth agape, eyes wide and blinking. I had to bite the inside of my lip to keep from snickering at him. Granted, about a year before, I'd been the one terrified of the massive skeleton, and Frances hadn't screamed like I had.

In the back of the cave, I discovered exactly what I'd feared. Those three perfect stones, red as any ruby, blue as any sapphire, and green as any emerald, had shattered. The remains of those stones lay scattered across the cave's floor. This was what I'd been afraid of seeing, and had absolutely no idea how to handle.

When I turned to leave, Frances was still staring up at the skeleton.

"Frances?" I said.

"Uh, yes?" he replied, not taking his eyes off the dragon.

"Remember me asking if you planned to save the damsel from a fate worse than death?"

"Yes. Why?"

"You might just have your chance."

That actually got his attention, and he looked at me. I waved my flute to the mouth of the cave. He blinked at me a few times and looked to where I'd gestured. Three drakes stood just outside the cave: one with scales red as any ruby, one with scales blue as any sapphire, and one with scales green as any emerald.

The Dragon Bone Flute

XII

Frances let out a sound partway between a squawk and a shriek. My heart sped up, my stomach felt as if I'd swallowed snow, and my breath came in short, quick blasts.

The shock I felt at these creatures looking back and forth between Frances and me faded much faster than I would have expected. I think part of it came from noticing that the little dragonlings looked massive at first, but after taking in the sight of them for a moment, I realized their bodies we actually no bigger than a large dog. They seemed to be so much larger because of their long necks and tails and how they spread their wings out and up. What really helped me remember myself was probably that day so many months before when I'd spoken to their mother's ghost. In hindsight now, I realize that the ghost might not have actually been about to do anything to me, being a ghost, but the idea of a dragon ghost scared me even more than three, potentially very hungry, drakes.

Frances pulled his knife and moved to place himself as well as he could between me and all three drakes. I couldn't help but laugh. I can't properly describe the ridiculousness of the sight. A scrawny boy just on the edge of being a man stood proud and defiant like a knight, with only a sturdy but tiny work knife to defend the damsel fair. I laughed louder when Frances turned to look at me. His expression had not a bit of fear in it. Rather, he looked at me with such self-righteous indignation that I couldn't help but laugh even harder and louder.

The drakes seemed puzzled by this. Their sinewy necks stretched out to look at me without Frances in the way. The blue drake cocked its head to the side as it regarded me, then it sniffed at the air, head rotating in all directions. After a few moments of watching us, the red and green drakes put their heads together. The red sucked in a lungful of air. I saw its chest expand as I heard the air rushing through its teeth.

All humor left me. In my mind, I saw it letting loose with a blast of flame. The fire might not be anything compared to the conflagration that its mother had used to kill the knight, but it would be enough to ignite poor Frances.

The flames didn't come. Instead, the drake let loose with a rolling series of sound that went low to high. I caught the feeling of the wonder of what new sight might be just around the next hill. The green responded with three notes, agreement with confusion.

I lifted my flute to my lips and played the same three notes the green had. Well, at least as best I could, considering the limitations of my flute. Funny, the thought of my flute being limited, as it had a greater range than any instrument I'd ever hear of.

All three heads whipped around to gaze at me, three sets of golden eyes staring at me, unblinking. The three of them piped a short sequence of notes back and forth in a rolling melody. Years before, a pair of minstrels had come to the town; one played a fiddle, and the other played a mandolin. Nearly every song they played was a bit of call and response, similar to this.

I played again, but this time, I did not copy exactly the sounds I heard. I added a bit of my own sound into the mix of notes.

That stopped them again. Their heads rose a bit, and they studied me.

We stood there in the cave, looking at each other. Their heads wove slightly side to side, and every few moments one would sniff.

"Frances," I whispered, "get behind me."

"But," he said in his normal tone of voice.

All three necks snapped like whips, and the three drakes focused their attention on Frances.

"Now," I whispered again.

How could I tell what they would make out of the hard and harsh tones of our spoken language? True, the dragon's ghost had spoken to me in my own tongue, but was that a thing of ghosts or something the dragon had learned after however many centuries it had lived?

"Right," Frances whispered.

He moved backward slowly, and I noticed that he did not lower his knife. I suppose it's lucky that the drakes were not old enough to know what that meant. Then again, their knowing might have saved some trouble later, and the course of my life would have been very different.

When Frances got behind me, I put the flute to my lips. I played my song. Not a specific song that I had written, but the song of how I came to be able to speak to the drakes. I played of three bullies who had stolen the voice from my throat, and my quest to retrieve it.

As the notes slogged through the songless winter, a chill breeze blew about, biting through my clothes. It gathered up twigs, leaves, and dust, swirling them around the mouth of the cave. When I came to when I found their mother and the knight, the debris flowed around me as the smoke had that first night in the tavern, the dragon and knight dancing and weaving around each other until finally killing each other. When this happened, the three drakes let out a high pitched whine of such utter sadness and loss that tears began to roll down my cheeks. I matched this note, joining in their pain. Then, slowly, I continued my song, slowly descending from that high-pitched wail to a low, sober span of notes as I slogged through that tedious winter, chewing and clawing into scraps of wood, trying to make a new voice for myself, to find a new song. I played of the wonder of finding my voice back here at the cave, and of how their mother's spirit had given me her blessing. I finished with nearly the same song I'd played the night before at Eric's request, of how spring emerges from winter, and how even with death, life continues.

As my final note trailed off, the drakes took up their own song. Gone was the pain they had cried earlier. Their song began with crisp notes that popped and cracked in the air, speaking of the wonder of breaking into a free and wide world. Together they wove a melody of hearing my song the night before and flitting through the air, in between trees, and up to the clouds searching for it. Such strange and wonderful things this world outside of the shells held. They ended with the rising sun, warm on their scales, and how they found something to eat, a cow or sheep, maybe.

After the drakes finished, all five of us, Frances, myself, and the drakes, stood regarding each other.

"This could be very bad," Frances said in a low voice, not quite a whisper.

I nodded. "We have to keep them hidden and teach them how to live."

"What?" Frances turned to me. "They're dragons. Oh, they might be young and cute now, but they're going to get bigger." To emphasize this he pointed back to the massive skeleton behind me. "We don't have any idea how long that could take."

A deep breath escaped through my pursed lips. He was right, though I'm sure it might take a bit of time before they really started to grow, and by that time, I might be able to convince them to move on to less populated areas. Even with Frances talking logically and reasonably about the drakes, I knew I could not turn my back on them. My song had brought them out. Somehow, someway, it had reached them out here, and pulling from my song of life coming from death, had caused them to hatch. Also, their mother had given me music again. I couldn't just abandon them. Of course, they might have been fine, they were dragons after all, but how could I be sure? No. I couldn't betray their mother and the gift she'd given me.

"I'm taking care of them," I said.

"But, Elzibeth," Frances started.

"But nothing." I had no interest in hearing whatever reasonable cautions or arguments he had against my doing this. "I'm doing this. I welcome any help you might give me, but only if you can do so without telling me what kind of foolish child I'm being, or anything even remotely close to that. If you can't do that, then go home, and by gods and goddesses, keep quiet about this."

"Of course I'm going to help you," he replied. Then he muttered under his breath, "It's the only way I can make sure you don't get yourself killed." I chose to ignore that comment.

XIII

Now, I could go into great details about the adventures we had that winter while we taught the dragons how to hunt and what to hunt, but those adventures have little actual bearing on my tale overall. The most important thing we did that winter was convince them to leave herds of sheep and cattle alone. This was our greatest challenge. Why should they ignore such easy prey, especially when winter snows made finding other food so much more challenging? When that question arose, I played for them again the song of their mother fighting the knight, and that if they hunted the humans' food, armies of hard-shelled humans would come seeking the drakes. By midwinter, we had finally managed to get them to understand. Little did I know that these lessons had come too late, that events had been set in motion the night I'd played the dirge at the wake for Hugh, Eric, and Gregory's father.

Let me now take you months later, a few weeks after the snows melted, as the first knight rode into the town. He came in the early afternoon. Frances and I saw him as we returned from the dragon's cave. The knight sat atop his massive horse, armor shining in the afternoon sun even under a layer of road dust. He took one of the three rooms above the tavern and started hunting dragons the next day.

Two days later, another knight came. Two came the day after. Within a fortnight, we'd lost track of the knights coming and going between our town and the others in the area. Word had traveled over the winter, as word does, and now dozens of armored soldiers – some knights, some just would-be heroes – had come seeking fame and glory by being the one to slay the dragon.

Frances and I did our best to remain as unobtrusive as possible. For Frances, it wasn't really a difficult task. For me, well, I had a reputation, and within the month, men in armor with swords on their hips came around asking me questions. I was, after all, the girl with the magic flute. Most of these men, the real knights mostly, respected that I didn't want to talk to them and let me be about my way. I contented myself with playing only in the middle of the night, hidden away in my room, and only with human songs I knew. I would not risk calling the drakes by playing a song from my heart. Such a song would surely bring them to the town, despite warnings to remain away.

One afternoon, as I was returning home from taking Father his midday meal, a man stepped in my way. His breast plate, while marked with nicks and dings – and one spot on his left shoulder had been pounded out after something had pierced it – wasn't poor quality as was the armor of some of the soldiers and fortune seekers who had come. We'd learned very quickly to judge the quality of the man by the quality of his armor – the better he kept it, the better the man. A few exceptions existed. In a small handful of the knights, the better he kept it meant the better he thought about himself. Still, while those few were pompous, and if the other knights hadn't been about they might have taken advantage of their station, they didn't get too out of hand in the company of their peers. The sellswords and mercenaries were a different breed altogether. At least every few days, the town put one of those men on trial for theft or for beating up one of the townsmen, and once, a knight killed a sellsword for rape even before anyone could even begin planning a trial.

"You're the girl with the flute," he said. It wasn't a question, more like an accusation.

"I play a flute now and then," I replied, trying to move around him. I'd gotten very good at the half-answer.

He moved to block my path.

"Please, sir," I said. "My mother is expecting me."

I curtsied and tried to move around him the other way. Again, he cut me off.

"You can take a moment to answer my questions. The sooner you do, the sooner you can return to your mother.

Now, does this power you have with music come from you or is it something in the flute?"

"I don't know what you mean, sir." I'd also become very good at lying, head down, gaze cast to the dust, a little curtsy added in, just for a little extra show. "I really must be going."

"No."

He grabbed my wrist. I fought against him, but his grip tightened around my forearm. The more I struggled, the more my skin burned against his gloved hand.

"You are going to stay and speak with me."

I dropped the basket I held and slapped him with my free hand. Even though his head snapped to the side, when he looked at me, red-cheeked, I could tell that I hadn't fazed him in the least. He looked from side to side, and when his face came back to look at me, the corners of his mouth turned upward in a humorless smile.

Pain flared all along the side of my head. The man let go of me, and I dropped to my knees. I blinked tears, and as my mind caught up with my senses, I remembered him slapping me. Part of me wished it had been Hugh to slap me again. Part of my reaction was due to the sudden pain, but a lot of it was just from the calculated way he'd made sure no one was watching and that he'd struck without anger, just to let me know that he could hurt me, and would hurt me.

He knelt down next to me on one knee, took up the basket I'd dropped, and placed it into my hands.

"You will tell me what I want to know. The only question is how much pain you, or perhaps your family, will suffer before then." He helped me to my feet. "Your mother is waiting. Run on home."

I did, just as he said. When I got there, I threw the basket into the kitchen as I passed and fell onto my bed weeping. Mother asked me what was wrong, but I wouldn't lift my face from my pillow. The side of my face had to be red and swelling. It still burned, still throbbed. She'd tell Father. Father would make me tell him what happened. Then Father would go looking for the man, and the man would hurt him, maybe kill him, because Father would start trouble and the man seemed used to more trouble than Father could ever make for him.

After a few moments of trying to comfort me and get some semblance of an explanation, Mother let me be. "If it's those three boys again, you let us know. We've got troubles enough these days without them causing more."

I remained there, face in my pillow, until I fell asleep.

Hours later, I awoke. The pain had retreated to a dull ache. Night had fallen, and my room was shrouded in darkness. Someone was tapping at my window. I sighed and stumbled to the window.

"What do you want, Frances?" I asked as I opened it.

"Not just Frances," the hard man from earlier said.

I tried to back away, but he grabbed me by the shoulder with more speed than I could fathom.

"Small town people are so easy," the man said. "For one small silver coin, Frances here led me right to your window."

I craned my neck and saw Frances' slight form in the shadows. I also saw three larger shadows coming up behind the man.

"Is this him?" Frances asked.

I nodded.

"Do it," Frances said, taking two large steps back.

One of the larger shadows rushed forward. The hard man frowned, released me, and began to turn. His hand went down to his belt. Before he could finish turning or draw his sword, a dull clang echoed in the night outside my window. The hard man staggered, shaking his head. The two other larger shadows came in. I saw Hugh, Eric, and Gregory swinging shovels again and again, beating the hard man about the arms, chest, and shoulders. He didn't have his breastplate on. Such a garment would have severely limited his stealth. I believe I heard bones snapping and cracking as the brothers beat on him, especially after he dropped to the ground.

"Enough," Frances said after a few moments. He knelt down next to the hard man. "You know nothing of us. We protect our own." Frances looked up to the brothers. "Take him somewhere and let him consider this evening."

Eric and Gregory each grabbed a foot and dragged the hard man into the night. Hugh marched a few paces after them, shovel held ready to strike.

"Are you alright?" Frances asked once they were gone.

I nodded. He reached in the window and caressed my cheek. Then he followed after the brothers.

I finally managed to get back to sleep, but not without wondering what had become of the hard man. Had they killed him? Part of me hoped that they had, but another part of me hoped that they had not taken themselves down that path. Yes, the brothers had been bullies, but I didn't want to think them capable of murdering someone.

XIV

The next day, I found Frances and was about to ask what had happened to the hard man when I heard someone snarl, "You!"

The hard man came around a corner and headed for us. He moved stiffly, and the left side of his face scrunched with pain every time he took a step with his left foot. His sword was in his hand. Frances and I both froze. Ambushing a soldier in the dark of night was one thing. Seeing the hard man coming toward you with a naked blade is another thing entirely.

Before he reached us, a knight stepped between us. Even with his back to us, I could tell it was a knight. His armor gleamed in the sunshine as he took a wide stance. His sword was out, and though the knight held it casually at his side, he stood in such a way that made me realize that he was prepared to use it.

"Hold," the knight said, his deep voice resonating with command.

"Stand aside, boy," the hard man said. "This doesn't concern you."

"Oh, but it does," the knight said. "While my peers have been hunting dragons, I've been hunting you. You're the one terrorizing young ladies looking for this girl with the flute. Well, I've caught you, and you've drawn steel against the innocent. Lay your sword down, never return, and I will spare your life."

The hard man tried to push past the knight. With even more speed than the hard man possessed, the knight had disarmed him and taken him off his feet. The knight placed the tip of his sword at the hard man's throat. The hard man's sword was a good three paces away.

"Now that you have laid your sword aside," the knight said, "you may comply with the rest of my request. If I ever see you within a hundred leagues of this town, your life is forfeit."

The knight backed away, keeping his sword pointed at the hard man. The hard man got to his feet with several grunts and groans.

"Thank you for my life, my lord," the hard man said, without a trace of hardness left in him, and then he left. I never saw him again, not that I remained in my home much longer than that.

The knight turned to us, Frances and me, and gave a slight bow. "I am Sir Phillip, and I am your servant, my lady."

Sir Phillip was beautiful. While he was a man, he was a young man, perhaps twenty or so. He had chestnut-colored hair and deep brown eyes that seemed to smile with a pure, genuine delight of life. I blushed at receiving the attention of such a man.

Sir Phillip sheathed his sword, and offered me his arm. "Shall I escort you home?"

I nodded dumbly and placed my arm in his. He took me home and introduced himself to my parents, explained what had happened, and assured them they need not fear the man any further. Father and Mother both insisted my savior stay for supper.

"No, no," Sir Phillip said. "I couldn't possibly impose."

But my parents would not be dissuaded. While my father and Sir Phillip argued politely about him staying for dinner, my mother was already putting another place setting at the table. In the end, I made the difference in swaying Sir Phillip.

"Please, Sir Phillip?" I said, looking up at him, doing my best to keep the color out of my cheeks. "It's the least we can do for you saving me from that man."

"How could I possibly refuse such beauty?" Sir Phillip put his hand to his chest and sighed. "But I insist you call me only Phillip. I've learned that the Sir part only really matters at court."

And so he joined us.

I spent most of the evening quiet and blushing. Father pestered him with questions about being a knight and more importantly about his prospects of starting a family. This made me cover my face with my hair. Of course it is every father's duty to see his daughter well married, but this was going too far. Sir Phillip was far too high above my station, beyond anything I could even dream of reaching. As it was, even though I was reaching the age of marriage, I hadn't really considered it, mostly because my music filled my thoughts almost every moment. Until the drakes had hatched, that is.

After dinner, as Mother and I cleaned the dishes, Father and Phillip retired to the front room. I did my best to listen in, and Mother didn't seem to mind that this made cleaning up take nearly three times longer than normal. They spoke of normal things, Father bragging mostly of what a wonderful young lady I was. Phillip replied to all the praises I received with some earnest variation of, "I had definitely noticed."

After a bit, Phillip interrupted Father, asking, "I've been following that man for some time. In each town, he keeps raving about a girl with a flute. That this girl knows the secrets of the dragons."

My heart sank into my stomach. I knew what was coming next, and that as much as I hated it, I couldn't do anything to stop it.

"Oh, that would indeed be Elzibeth," Father replied. "She has a flute that seems to be magical. Made it herself last winter. Seen and heard the strangest things when she's played it." Then his voice rose. "Elzibeth, get your flute and play something for our guest."

I took a deep breath and chewed the inside of my cheek. How much trouble would I get into if I refused? Then again, how many questions would it raise if I did refuse? I knotted my hair into my fists until finally, I relented. I went to my room, got my flute out from under my pillows, and took it to the front room.

Phillip stood when I entered, his gaze falling on my flute.

"That's quite beautiful," he said.

"It's just a plain flute," I said.

"Sometimes ordinary things hold the greatest beauty," Phillip replied. "A flower, a sunset, or a flute made by loving hands. I've never seen that kind of wood before. Is it native to this area?"

I said nothing at first. I'd not mentioned it to anyone since that day Hugh had broken my grandfather's flute, but I heard the whispers and the rumors people spoke when they thought I was too far away to hear. They all knew I had claimed it was a dragon bone. My refusal to talk about it might have been part of the fuel to fire this local piece of gossip. Even in that moment, I couldn't speak of it.

"Girl," Father said, "our guest asked you a question."

I just stared into the fire. I opened my mouth and tried to speak, but could not. In the end, I gave Sir Phillip a polite curtsy and fled to my room. Behind me, Father apologized over and over for my rudeness.

"Oh, think nothing of it," Phillip said. "She's had quite the time of it over that flute. Were I in her place and some raving mad mercenary came at me with a sword because of my flute, I don't think I'd be inclined to share much about it, either. I'm just glad I managed to intercede when I did. Well, I should be off. I need to make sure that villain is actually gone."

With some shuffling and much thanks from Mother and Father, Phillip left. Thankfully, Father seemed to heed Phillip's words and did not come to admonish me for my behavior.

Later that night, I heard a tapping on my window. Frances. I'd forgotten all about him. I struck myself in the forehead several times and wondered if I might have the will to actually succeed in smothering myself with my pillow.

Feeling like the worst friend in the world, I went over and opened the window.

"Frances, I'm—"

"Who is Frances?" Phillip asked.

I jumped back a bit, flailing in my surprise.

"I'm sorry," Phillip said. "I didn't mean to scare you. I just wanted to hear you play something on this flute. Just one song. Please?"

So there I stood, alone in my night clothes, moon and starlight shining through my window. The most handsome man I'd seen in my whole life asking me to play for him. Even in the center of a scene that seemed straight out of a fairy story, I was still going to refuse, until he looked at me and asked just above a whisper, "Please, Elzibeth?"

He spoke my name as if it were a holy benediction, and I was his. He could have asked for my virginity then, and I would have gladly given it to him.

I took my flute and placed it to my lips and played "Lovers at the Well." It's a short little song with a dance set to it. Even under the enchantment of this moment, I knew better than to let the music fly free. Still, I did embellish the song a bit, adding just a bit of a twirl and an extra few notes at the end. What could it hurt to impress the knight a bit? After all, he'd been so kind.

When the song was over, he reached in through the window. I placed my hand in his, and he drew me closer, never taking his eyes from mine.

"Thank you," Phillip said, and kissed my knuckles.

I shivered from the touch of it. He pulled me even closer to him. In two steps, I came face to face with him, only my wall separating us. He leaned in and kissed me, his lips to my lips.

Phillip left after the kiss, and I went to bed. Again, I'd forgotten all about Frances.

And I'll leave the kiss at that. I still have so many emotions wrapped up in that kiss, from the time it happened, to the arguments I've had with Frances about it, to how I felt about it after the events of the next day. No, I will say this: today the strongest emotion I feel is the shame at how much that kiss hurt Frances. He'd been watching from the shadows, with Hugh, Eric, and Gregory, to make sure I wasn't going to be bothered again. Even today, I wonder if he ever truly forgave me for that betrayal that was not a betrayal, for no words had been spoken, no agreements made.

XV

I looked for Phillip the next day but couldn't see him anywhere. I also didn't see Frances, but I didn't know that because he was the furthest thing from my mind. By the time I took the midday meal to my father in the fields, I'd begun to lose hope of seeing Phillip again. A deep ache began to form in my chest, just below my heart.

As I returned home, I heard cries and cheers from the other side of the town. Some few people were even sounding horns. I hurried that way, hoping that the excitement might draw Phillip. When I got there, I saw that it was Sir Phillip who was drawing the excitement. He rode into town, a pack horse trailing behind him carrying a slumped form, red as any ruby. Everyone in the town, commoners, sellswords, and knights alike were cheering Sir Phillip. He grinned, reveling in the attention, waving his bloody sword in the air for all to see. Then I noticed the blood on his armor. He had transformed into the most hideous creature I had ever seen.

A burning fury replaced the growing ache. My jaw ached from clenching back my scream of outrage. My mere screams would not be enough.

I pushed through the crowd to stand in front of Sir Phillip. I took my flute and placed it to my lips. Normally, in those days with the knights and soldiers and all, I'd taken to leaving my flute hidden at home. That day, I'd carried it around with me, just on the off chance I found Sir Phillip and he wanted me to play again.

"Hello, Elzibeth," Sir Phillip said. "I wanted to thank you—"

As he spoke, I placed the flute to my lips and blew out a low note that matched my anger, the fury in my heart, the heat of rage as red as any ruby. The sound of it drowned out his words. People around us stepped back.

Phillip shouted something at me, but I played louder. I wanted him to understand the hurt he had caused me. I wanted him to know the hellfire of my scorn, and the only way I knew how to do that was through my flute.

People moved back again. I saw Sir Phillip mouth my name, but I couldn't hear him over my anger and the sound of my single, prolonged note. He said something else, but I kept playing. Soon, his mouth opened in a scream. His horse reared up. Sir Phillip fell to the ground, writhing in the mud. The mud steamed and bubbled where he rolled in it. And now the smell of cooking meat filled the air.

I stopped playing. Sir Phillip had gone from screams of agony to whimpers. His thrashing turned to twitching as the skin on his neck, where it touched his armor, blistered and peeled. A few moments later, both his twitching and whimpering ended. The only sound in the wake of his death was the popping and hissing of his skin and the mud he lay in.

Before anyone else could recover from the shock, I fled. Long and fast and hard, I ran. At first, I had no idea where I was headed, but soon I found myself approaching the dragon's cave. There, I found the green and blue drakes wailing in their sadness.

I joined them in their song, adding my flute to their dirge. Then I shifted the song from one of weeping loss to one of flight. I played again of humans with their hard shells and long claws that pierce even dragon hides. I played of the armies coming to find the drakes and that they would not be safe in these hills. I played until the two drakes took to the sky and flew north until I could see them no longer and heard no more of their sorrowful song.

Then, I fled.

XVI

I ran again, this time without a destination. I walked and ran the rest of that day, through the night, and all the next day. I couldn't stop. That the tale of Elzibeth and her cursed flute would be told, I had no doubt, and it would grow with the telling. I needed to stay ahead of it if I was to have any hope.

As the sun set that second day, my mind caught up with my emotions. The realization that I'd killed a man hit me. I cried all through that night, but I didn't stop running, not until the small hours of that morning when despair and exhaustion overcame me. I had just enough presence of mind to crawl into a thicket to sleep out of open sight before my eyes closed.

For a month I traveled, avoiding any contact with humans. I ate what plants I could find in the wild. At times, the flute tempted me. I could have used it to lure a rabbit or some other small game into a trap, and I could eat well on meat. That I had nothing to start a fire with didn't bother me. I was half-crazed from hunger and grief. Even raw meat would have been better than another day of wild berries and grubs scavenged from a fallen log.

One morning, a week into my second month, I woke and knew I was not alone. First it was the smell, cooking bacon and oatmeal. Then I heard the bacon sizzling in a pan and the fire popping and crackling. I bolted into a crouch, ready to run.

"Good morning," Frances said.

I opened my mouth, and though it had only been five weeks since I'd spoken to another person, it also seemed a thousand lifetimes ago.

"Are you hungry?" he asked.

I nodded.

He gave me a bowl with oatmeal and bacon in it. I ate them greedily, and he gave me more. This second helping went down just as quickly. Frances watched me, patiently, as he ate his own breakfast.

"How did you find me?" I asked.

"The blue drake," he said. "Don't worry. Now that he knows you're safe with me, he's going to stay away from people."

"How do you know?" I asked. I'd always been the one to translate between Frances and the drakes.

"He actually speaks our language fairly well," Frances replied. "We knew you needed taking care of. I've been following as best I could, while they've been scouting for you. They aren't big enough to carry me yet, or I would have caught up with you several weeks ago."

"Why didn't they let me know?" I asked, thinking about all the meat I could have been eating if they'd helped.

"The drakes didn't want you to be mad at them for disobeying you. Anyhow, they are gone now, gone far away from people, now that I'm here."

"I don't need taking care of," I said, though my words sounded hollow in the face of my ragged clothes and the smell of bacon grease on the air.

"Of course not."

And so we traveled together for several years.

We never spoke of my kissing Sir Phillip, or what I'd done to him the next day. We rarely spoke of the drakes, and when we did, it was only by their color, as in, "Remember when Green broke through the ice trying to land that one day?" We spoke of Red least often. Every time we did, I would cry for hours afterward.

Finally, we came to a place where we thought we might live, a city far beyond any place that had heard of Elzibeth and her cursed flute. We married and started raising a family. I never played the flute again and did my best to stay away from anything that might tempt me to take it back up again. I don't know, but part of me believes that a pair of dragons, blue as any sapphire and green as any emerald, are out there, waiting to hear the call of that flute on the wind.

XVII

Elzibeth left the story of her childhood on her kitchen table amongst the candlesticks. It had taken her so much longer to write it than she'd expected. There was so much in that tale, more than she'd been able to put into the words. Then again, she wasn't a poet or a storyteller. She'd been a musician many miles away and years ago, but that was a different kind of thing altogether.

After completing the tale, she'd gone into her small garden behind the house. It reminded her of home, of her mother's vegetables, and of her father working in the fields. By the light of a single candle, Elzibeth had dug up the map case wrapped in oilcloth. She'd taken it up the stairs to the room she'd shared with her husband for their entire marriage. Oh, how she missed him. She missed him even more than the music. If she hadn't had him, the music would have overpowered her caution, but that's how it is with love: It gives us the strength to do what we could normally never do.

Lying in bed, Elzibeth took the flute out of the map case. She caressed it, letting her fingers become familiar with it once more. She had no idea how long she sat into the night, reacquainting herself with her old friend, just as she'd never really had any idea as a child how long she'd sat in a field playing her music.

Finally, Elzibeth raised the flute to her lips and played. She played as if she hadn't had the flute buried in the garden for decade upon decade.

She played for hours of the wonder and magic that her life had known. She played of three little drakes and one brave boy who grew into a braver man willing to share his life with her. She played of the sorrow she'd caused him with an unwitting kiss, and the sorrow she'd caused her parents by vanishing, and the sorrow she felt for never really feeling sorry that she'd murdered the man who had used her to kill her friend. Finally, she let the last notes of her song echo of how she'd missed the music.

The song ended. For a time, Elzibeth, her bones weary, sat in the silence that always seemed to follow the end of a song. It lingered on, and on, until she heard a tapping at the window.

Tap. Tap. Tap. Quiet.

Tap. Tap. Tap. Quiet.

Elzibeth got up from the bed, went to the window, and opened it.

A single eye filled the window. It was blue as any Sapphire.

"We've been waiting for you to sing again."

Please enjoy this excerpt of the second book in *The Saga of the Dragon Bone Flute.*

I

We all look back and search for those moments that define ourselves, the moments where we made a choice, and in making that choice, we affect all other choices to follow and we close off any chance of avoiding whatever fate comes with that choice. I didn't believe that then, back when I was young and believed myself immortal, as the young do, and had the luxury of believing that coincidence and chance controlled my destiny rather than taking responsibility for my actions. My name is Killian. I will not give you my family name, for I have family that survives me. While I hope this account finds its way into one of my descendants' hands, as my grandmother's journal found its way into mine, I cannot be sure. And so, I will protect my family from the choices I have made, and the enemies that came along with those choices.

Now, I was speaking of moments and choices that change the course of our lives. If any one moment could be said to be the turning point in my life, I'd like to be able to say it was when I decided – against, I might add, the wishes and warnings of my parents, grandparents, siblings, and cousins – to explore the abandoned farmstead of my great grandmother. But it was not that day when I decided I was old enough – this happened to be my ten-and-fifth naming day – to command my own fate, and sneak out early one morning with the forbidden farmstead as my solitary goal. It's true, the moment I left the yard, walking through the gate without being called back, was a shift in my destiny, where all further actions and choices moved me toward becoming a hero, trickster, villain, madman, wanderer, fugitive, prince, hermit, and friend to legends, and all that before my ten-and-sixth name day.

But it was not that day, and it was not that choice.

The major snows had melted, and most of the village had gathered together in the tavern as was the tradition when spring began to creep back into the world. And as I neared my ten-and-fifth naming day, I sat alone in a corner. Now I was an oddity in the village. For whatever reason, I'd been born at a time of scarce births. Then several hard winters in a row had claimed the other children close to my age. So I considered myself too old to any longer tolerate sitting at the long table with the children – the eldest of them was three years younger than I was. Oh I'd tried to join with the adults, but I was not quite old enough for them to actually count me one of them. I'm sure my small stature didn't help. Without any peers close to my own age, the corner was the place I hid, mostly so I wouldn't suffer the humiliation of having my small beer taken away and then get herded back to shepherd over the children.

Alone and melancholy, trying to take solace in having a tankard of the weakest brew offered in the tavern, it took me a moment to realize someone was standing next to me. I looked up. My uncle, called Daft Uncle Ian by the village when he wasn't listening – even by those who weren't related to him – looked down at me.

"May I sit?" Uncle Ian asked.

I scooted over, making room on the bench. It took a bit for him to settle down next to me. He'd injured his leg in a war long past. Most of the village thought that's where he'd also gone daft, that he'd damaged his brain in the same cavalry charge that had crippled his leg.

Once he sat, bad leg stretched out before him, he took a long drink from his mug, stared into the fire and began to hum. I recognized the tune, "The Beggar King." It was one of my favorites. Before he finished even the first verse, he stopped humming and spoke to me.

"We're quite the pair," Uncle Ian said. "They all think us both wandering away from our senses. Don't bother arguing. I know what they say about me. And you…well…you might say that they think you're a bit daft for overstepping yourself and trying to join them before they invite you as has always been the way of it."

He took a sip from his tankard. I took a sip from mine.

"Here," he said, handing me his drink and taking mine. "I'm fool enough to have had one of these, much less be starting on my third. None of this lot will help me home tonight, and I've no need to be stumbling around in the dark trying to remember which home is mine. Just be sure you don't let your parents catch you with that mug of Highhill Dark."

"No, sir," I said.

Then I took a drink, a healthy-sized one.

The full flavor of it washed over my tongue and settled in my stomach with a weight that was at the same time warm and comforting and nauseating. A few moments later, my head swam. I could definitely grow to like this.

"You think they won't let you join them because you're still too young," Uncle Ian said.

I nodded.

"Not true." He drank. "They're afraid of you."

"Me?" I asked, my voice rising more than it normally would have, even considering my surprise at Uncle Ian's statement. I lowered it to a whisper. "Why would anyone be afraid of me?"

"You know that song you like so much?" he asked. "The one you're always playing or singing as you go about your chores and such."

"The Beggar King?" I asked. I had several such, but I was sharp enough, even back then, to see some things right in front of my face.

"The Beggar King," he replied. "It was her favorite song."

"Whose favorite song?" I asked.

"You remind them of her. Too much, you remind them. Of her."

"Who, her?"

Ian leaned close to my ear. "Heeeerrr." His breath tickled my ear and neck. His breath stank of beer and stew.

I thought for what might have been a few moments. Thinking had suddenly become a more difficult task than I remembered it being.

"You have the look of her," Uncle Ian said, "More than anyone in the family. Short, wiry, shock of flame on your head that some people call hair. I've heard my parents whisper that you have her manner, too. Stubborn, proud, and a flat refusal to let anyone dictate your life for you."

"Oh." I took another drink of my Highhill Dark, though not as healthy a swallow as my first taste. "That her."

Uncle Ian was speaking of my great-grandmother Elzibeth. She and my great grandfather Frances had come to the village when they were only slightly older than I was. They'd picked a plot of land on the very edge of the village and settled there. Stories about them from that point disagree. One of the most fanciful is the reason most folk think of Uncle Ian as Daft Uncle Ian.

"I saw it happen, you know," he said.

"I know," I said. "You've told me before."

"So I have," Uncle Ian said, "but I haven't told you everything. I haven't ever told anyone everything."

I took another drink, bracing myself for the story to come. Everyone knew the best thing to do was to sit quietly when Ian started in on this, let him get on with his tale, and pray that it was one of the shorter versions he told.

"It was shortly after I'd come home from the war. My leg still hurt with stabbing pains all the time back then, not the simple ache I feel now. I was up late, biting my lips to keep from whimpering and crying so my parents could sleep. They took good care of me and didn't need their crippled son keeping them up at all hours. It was a warm night, so I had my shutters open. I might as well enjoy the summer breeze and the peace that comes with the quiet of the world at sleep."

Ian took a drink of the small beer he'd taken from me.

"You've heard this before," Ian said, "all about Daft Uncle Ian and how he saw dragons that carried Grandmother Elzibeth away. But you've never heard it with that," he pointed to the tankard he'd given me. "That's why you're pretending to listen, so you can enjoy that tasty bit of drink. But here's what I've never told anyone. Before the dragons came, I heard music. Flute music."

I sat up straight and turned to give Uncle Ian my full attention. This was a new part of the story.

"Got your attention, did that?" he asked. "I thought it might. Have you ever wondered why so many of the older folk in the village seem to shy away whenever you pick up that flute you bought from the peddler a few years ago?"

I shook my head.

"They fear it, you playing any musical instrument, but most of all a flute."

"Why?"

He smiled at me in a way that I'd never seen Uncle Ian smile before. It was the smile that someone gave to someone else who was so sick or injured that they might never recover, a smile while trying to spare the terrible news as long as possible. He reached for the tankard of Highhill Dark. I gave it over without protest. As much as I enjoyed the effect and was even growing accustomed to the potent taste, young people of the village, even when they were close to their ten-and-fifth name day, did not disobey and disrespect their elders.

"You've gotten fairly good." He took a long drink of the Highhill Dark. "That's even more reason why you scare them."

I tried to wait patiently, but he seemed unwilling to continue. I tried to content myself by listening to other conversations, but no one was close enough for me to hear them clearly above the din of the rest of the tavern. I hummed through a complete round of, "The Beggar King" and two other songs quietly to myself. After that, I waited for what seemed like forever, I couldn't help but speak up.

"Uncle Ian, why does my flute playing scare them?"

He leaned close and whispered "Listen well, young Killian. I will not tell this again. I probably shouldn't now, but I think you should know what kind of door you've opened and are getting ready to walk through."

"Does it have something to do with you hearing flute music the night Grandmother Elzibeth got carried off?"

"You're getting ahead of my story, boy." Uncle Ian glared at me even as he drank again. "Don't ever get ahead of the story. That's the problem with you musicians. Everything is so fast for you. Put everything together in a song that takes only a few minutes, and everything repeats over and over and over. You've got no appreciation for the beginning, middle, and end of things."

"I'm sorry Uncle Ian." Part of me couldn't believe I was apologizing for this. He was on the edge, and I suspect he hadn't been honest with me when he'd handed me the Highhill Dark. I should have walked away. I almost did. But then that bit about the flute music held me to the bench. I'd heard him tell this story countless times, but this was the first time he'd ever mentioned any music. "I'll listen quietly, and let you tell the story the proper way.

"Good on you then, lad." Uncle Ian patted me on the back. "Good on you."

We sat there for a while, him drinking, me waiting. And I waited quietly, so that I didn't upset him and lose this tale. I feared if Uncle Ian walked away from this telling, I'd never have a chance to hear it again.

Finally, he put the tankard aside, put his arm around me, and drew me in close.

"I heard it floating down from Grandmother Elzibeth's cottage. It was beautiful…more haunting and beautiful than anything I've ever heard…not from any minstrel coming through on his way from one place to another…beautiful enough to break your heart with the knowing that magic had come to the world and the world had scorned it…even killed a part of it…and then…the magic left…fled really…and all because we chased it away.

"And while I heard that song, my leg stopped hurting…for the first time since I fell from that horse, my leg stopped hurting. I could walk. When I got outside of the cottage, I found I could run.

"That's when I saw them…coming down from the sky…even in the moonlight I saw them…one green as any emerald and one blue as any sapphire…almost as if they radiated the colors of their scaly hides…then the music stopped.

"Pain flared in my leg again. I fell to the road and rolled behind a cart. I nearly bit my tongue in half to keep from crying out. The last thing I wanted was to attract their attention, but that also didn't stop me from watching from the shadows under that cart. I watched them pull the roof off Grandmother Elzibeth's cottage, set that roof down, reach into her cottage, pick her up, and carry her off. The green one scooped her up out of the cottage and placed her right down on the blue one, just in front of its wings.

"And that's the last anyone ever saw of Grandmother Elzibeth. And that's why we moved the village. Don't let anyone else tell you otherwise, boy. Though none else will admit it, I was not the only one to see dragons that night. There was much talk of it during the days we moved.

Small-minded folk, most the people here are, thinking that moving half a day south would save them if the dragons ever came back looking to cause mischief, or worse. I knew better from my travels, but they wouldn't hear any of my advice, and it's not like I was in any shape with my leg the way it is to move on myself."

He took another drink, finishing the mug.

"But you'd heard all that before," Uncle Ian said, "about the dragons and such, isn't that right, boy?"

"Yes, sir," I replied.

"But not the music."

"No, sir," I said. "Not about the music."

"And there's something else," Uncle Ian said. He leaned in very close and whispered so low I could barely hear him. "Do you want to hear it?"

I nodded.

"As those two dragons flew up into the night, I saw something drop. I couldn't tell what, but I saw something small, flashing white in the moonlight fall from the sky moments after they rose out of sight. After that, sometimes, when the wind was just right, a solitary note would hang on the wind, and my leg wouldn't hurt. First happened the day after they took her. That was part of the reason they fled, the cowards. That one note pushed them over the edge of reason. I argued against it. They wouldn't hear me. Silly, superstitious folk. Not that I blame them overly much. I'd been like them before I left for the wars. Wish I hadn't. Then I wouldn't have this leg, and I wouldn't know what idiots my family and neighbors are, that I'd been too, once upon a time."

"What's going on here?" a deep voice asked.

Both Uncle Ian and I jumped.

My father stood behind us, glaring down.

"What nonsense are you filling my son's head with?" my father asked.

"Nothing, Father," I replied. "He was just telling me his story," I added with as bored a tone as I could manage, "again."

Father looked at Uncle Ian and me, back and forth several times. The disapproval of that gaze pressed down upon me. When dealing with my uncle, I was, like many of the children of the village, caught between two expectations: Do not spend too much time with Daft Uncle Ian, and do not under any circumstances be rude to your elders.

"Well, your mother's tired," Father said at last. "We're going home."

"Yes, Father," I said. "Thank you for telling me the story, Uncle Ian."

Uncle Ian nodded. Father led me away. Mother was waiting for us by the door.

"How many times have I told you?" Father asked. "Stay away from your Uncle Ian."

I knew he didn't really expect an answer. Even at ten and four, I'd gotten fairly good at understanding the difference between questions my elders expected me to answer and the questions they were merely asking to drive home a point I should have already gotten through my thick skull and put into practice. I just kept my eyes on the floor and nodded.

When we joined my mother outside, Father cuffed me on the back of the head so hard I took a couple of staggering steps forward to keep my balance.

"Look at me, Killian!" Father snapped.

I quickly wiped the welling tears from my eyes before turning to face him.

"Your Uncle can be charming and warm and exciting with his stories of dragons and his adventures during the war," Father said. "But he's also dangerous. Best not to talk to him so he can't be putting crazy ideas into your head."

"Yes, Father," I said.

Father flicked me on the nose. "Stop giving me the answers you think I want to hear, especially now that you're becoming a young man. There's no telling what he might try to talk you into doing for him. Promise me you won't do anything foolish."

"I know, Father," I said, blinking from the pain. "I know what my responsibilities are and where my duty lies."

What I didn't say was that Daft Uncle Ian had treated me more like an adult this evening than my father ever had. I also learned long ago when to keep the hole under my nose closed.

Daft Uncle Ian hadn't talked me into doing anything, but my father certainly had.

ABOUT THE AUTHOR

M Todd Gallowglas invented tea time, the horseless carriage, and sliced bread, and the internet. He is the reason why we have bubbles in beer, and he was also the first person to reach both the West Pole AND the East Pole. Bigfoot and the Loch Ness Monster are in his writing group. "Outstanding imaginative story telling," he reports on their work, "But they sometimes struggle with tense and verb congogation." He has written one thousand highly regarded books under several dozen nom de plumes, and hired actors to portary those nom de plumes at signings, conferences, and in interviews. a team of experts is presently attempting to grasp their meaning. Gallowglas currently resides in Blarney, Ireland where he raises wolf hound-corgie mixes when not distilling whiskey and playing whist with Phileas Fogg, Rudolf Rassendyll, Elizbeth Bennet, and Dr. James Watson.

OTHER BOOKS BY
M TODD GALLOWGLAS

Legacy of the Dragon Bone Flute
Legend of the Dragon Bone Flute
Challenges of the Dragon Bone Flute
Dirge of the Dragon Bone Flute

Halloween Jack and the Devil's Gate
Halloween Jack and the Curse of Frost
Halloween Jack and the Red Emperor

Lullabies for Dungeon Crawlers,
Advanced Lullabies for Dungeon Crawlers

Stopwatch Stories
Writing 365

My Journey in Creative Reading

Made in the USA
Middletown, DE
06 February 2023